NO RAIN,
NO FLOWERS

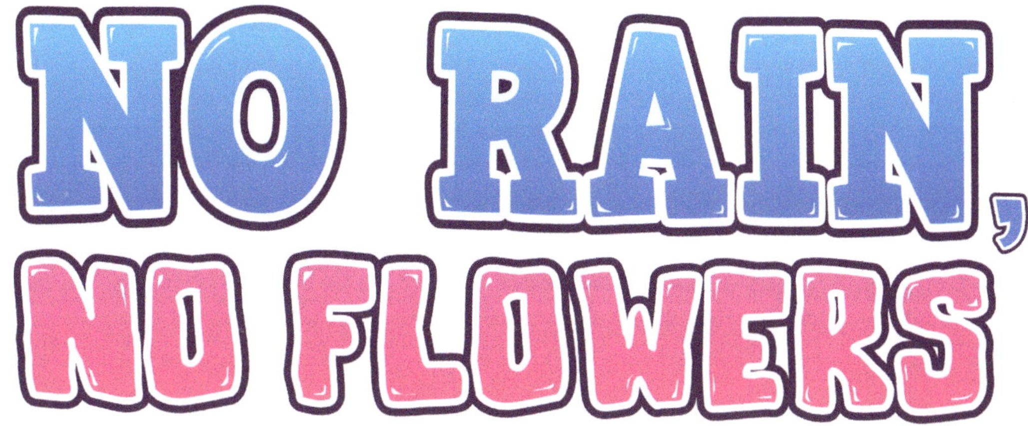

NO RAIN, NO FLOWERS

KARON DEXTRA

ReadersMagnet, LLC

This is for **Braelynn**, **Kennedy**, **Lavender**, **Stephan Jr.**, **Chris Jr.**, **Krystal**, **Donte**, **Deanna**, and **Sadé**.

To my loving husband **Stephan Sr.**,

Thank you for choosing me every day. I choose you too, and I love you.

To my dad **Chris Sr.**,

You have always been enough. Thank you for all that you do, we love you.

In loving memory of our heroes, **Karen Searvance-Council** and **Joseph Jean-Claude Dextra**.

Thank you Gammie and Pop Pop. To our Dextra family, we thank you for your love and continuous support. We love you.

"To my loving wife, there isn't anything you can't do. I'm so proud of you!!!"

Love,
Steph

Mommy Bonnie Butterfly went out for a morning fly. Little Bray Butterfly sees Mommy cry.

"When Mommy Bonnie is sad, I am sad too.
I want to help. What can I do?"

"Maybe Mommy Bonnie has fallen. Maybe she is hurt.
I'll give her my dolly. I think that should work."

"That's so very kind my dear Little Bray,
But thank you, no thank you, I'll be okay."

"Maybe Mommy Bonnie is sleepy and cranky.
When I need a nap she gives me my blankie."

"That's so very kind my dear Little Bray,
But thank you, no thank you, I'll be okay."

"Oh, I know what it could be. Mommy
Bonnie must be hungry.
I bet she would really like a snack,
I love some fresh pollen after a nap."

"That's so very kind my dear Little Bray,
But thank you, no thank you, I'll be okay."

"Mommy Bonnie is still crying. What could it be?
Mommy Bonnie won't you please tell me?"

The clouds start to fill and it begins to rain.
"My dear Little Bray, let Mommy explain."

"Most times I am happy, sometimes I get mad,
but just like you, Mommy also gets sad."

"You're so very thoughtful to help when I'm crying.
It isn't your fault, but thank you for trying."

"Sadness comes, but it doesn't last. It's
just like the rain, it surely will pass.
And after the rain there's beautiful weather,
like after my tears I feel so much better."

"So just think of my tears as a little rain shower,
And if there is no rain, then there are no flowers."

10620 Treena Street, Suite 230
San Diego, California,
CA 92131 USA
www.readersmagnet.com
1.619.354.2643
Copyright 2021 All Rights Reserved